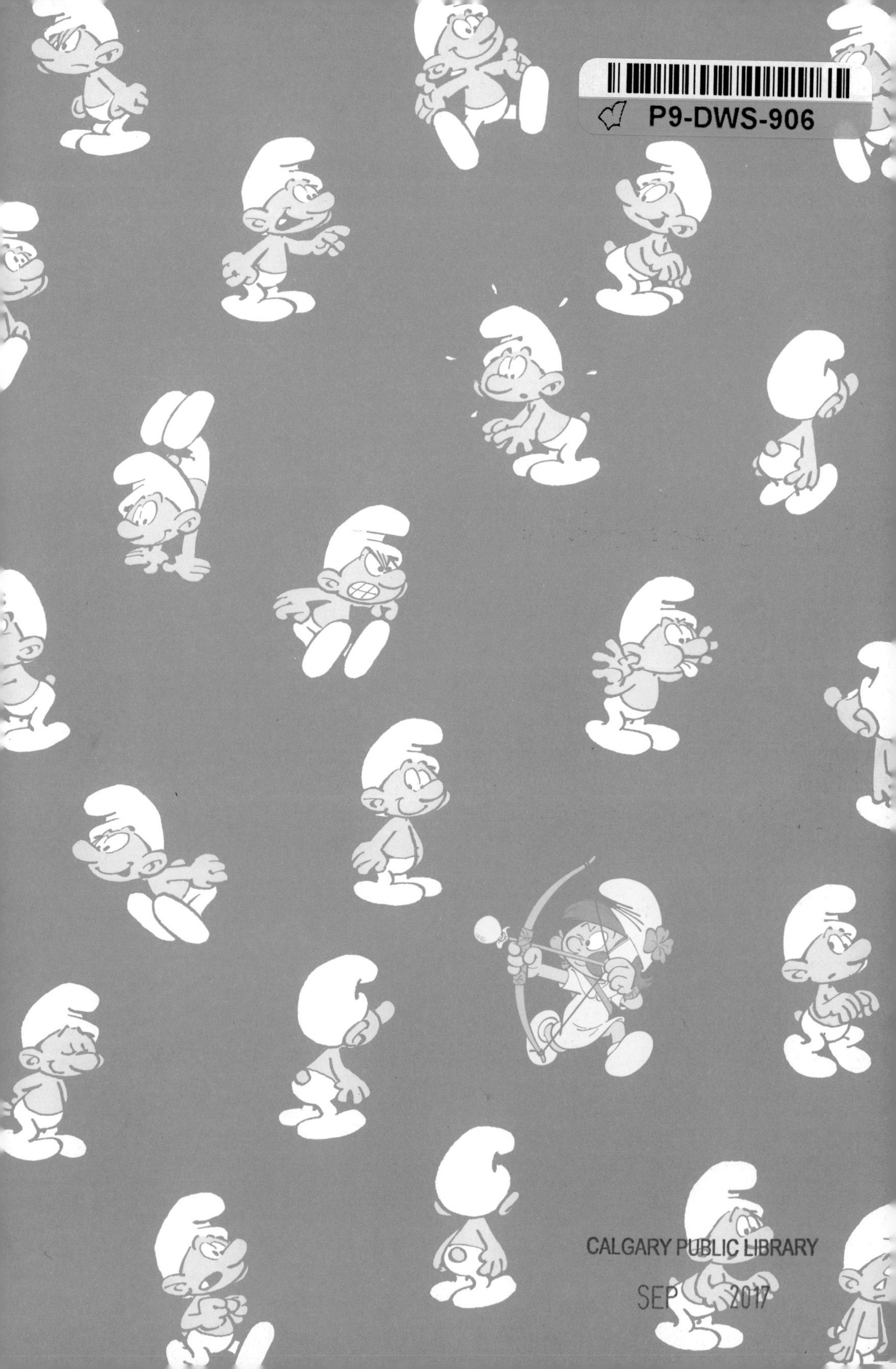

# SMURFS
## THE VILLAGE BEHIND THE WALL

Peyo

# the SMURFS™

## THE VILLAGE BEHIND THE WALL

Then she draws her bow as taut as she can...

...and, with precision, shoots her arrow...

TZING

...into a tree on the other side of the rapids.

TCHAK

Just you wait and smurf!

Look out below!

That goofball doesn't know who he's dealing with!

A **SMURFS** GRAPHIC NOVEL BY *Peyo*

WITH THE COLLABORATION OF
LUC PARTHOENS AND ALAIN JOST — SCRIPT
ALAIN MAURY, JEROEN DE CONINCK, MIGUEL DIAZ AND LAURENT CAGNIAT — ART
PAOLO MADDELENI — COLOR

### PAPERCUTZ™
NEW YORK

# SMURFS GRAPHIC NOVELS AVAILABLE FROM PAPERCUTZ

THE SMURFS graphic novels are available in paperback for $5.99 each and in hardcover for $10.99 each, except for THE SMURFS #21, THE SMURFS #22, and THE VILLAGE BEHIND THE WALL which are $7.99 each in paperback and $12.99 each in hardcover, at booksellers everywhere. You can also order online at papercutz.com. Or call 1-800-886-1223, Monday through Friday, 9 – 5 EST. MC, Visa, and AmEx accepted. To order by mail, please add $4.00 for postage and handling for first book ordered, $1.00 for each additional book and make check payable to NBM Publishing. Send to: Papercutz, 160 Broadway, Suite 700, East Wing, New York, NY 10038.

THE SMURFS graphic novels are also available digitally wherever e-books are sold.

PAPERCUTZ.COM

## SMURFS THE VILLAGE BEHIND THE WALL

SMURF™ ©Peyo - 2017 - Licensed through Lafig Belgium - www.smurf.com

English translation copyright © 2017 by Papercutz.
All rights reserved.

"Brainy Smurf's Walk"
BY PEYO
WITH THE COLLABORATION OF
ALAIN JOST FOR THE SCRIPT,
JEROEN DE CONINCK FOR ARTWORK,
PAOLO MADDELENI FOR COLOR.

"Challenges for Hefty Smurf"
BY PEYO
LUC PARTHOENS FOR THE SCRIPT,
ALAIN MAURY FOR ARTWORK,
PAOLO MADDELENI FOR COLOR.

"Clumsy Smurf's Dragonfly"
BY PEYO
LUC PARTHOENS FOR THE SCRIPT,
LAURENT CAGNIAT FOR ARTWORK,
PAOLO MADDELENI FOR COLOR.

"The Squash Smurfs"
BY PEYO
LUC PARTHOENS FOR THE SCRIPT,
ALAIN MAURY FOR ARTWORK,
PAOLO MADDELENI FOR COLOR.

"Smurflily Strange World"
BY PEYO
WITH THE COLLABORATION OF
ALAIN JOST FOR THE SCRIPT,
MIGUEL DIAZ FOR ARTWORK,
PAOLO MADDELENI FOR COLOR.

Joe Johnson, SMURFLATIONS
Adam Grano, SMURFIC DESIGN
Janice Chiang, LETTERING SMURFETTE
Calvin Louie, LETTERING ASSISTANT SMURF
Matt. Murray, SMURF CONSULTANT
Sasha Kimiatek, SMURF COORDINATOR
Jeff Whitman, ASSISTANT MANAGING SMURF
Jim Salicrup, SMURF-IN-CHIEF

PAPERBACK EDITION ISBN: 978-1-62991-782-5
HARDCOVER EDITION ISBN: 978-1-62991-783-2

PRINTED IN CHINA MARCH 2017 BY WKT CO. LTD.

Papercutz books may be purchased for business or promotional use. For information on bulk purchases please contact Macmillan Corporate and Premium Sales Department at (800) 221-7945 x5442.

DISTRIBUTED BY MACMILLAN
FIRST PAPERCUTZ PRINTING

## SMURFWILLOW (WILLOW)

Smurfwillow is the magnanimous leader of Smurfy Grove. The decision-maker of the group, Willow has raised her girls to be tough warriors, ready for whatever dangers they may face in the forest. She also has great knowledge of plants and botany, mixing flowers into potions to create healing elixirs.

# SMURFSTORM (STORMY)

Smurfy Grove is protected thanks to their toughest warrior, Smurfstorm. Good with a bow and arrow and quick to jump into any problem, Smurfstorm is fierce...and fiercely loyal to her friends.

# SMURFBLOSSOM (BLOSSOM)

Smurfblossom loves to talk. She can talk about anything to anyone and just talk and talk and talk. Granted with the gift of gab, Blossom can always see the positive side to any situation.

# SMURFLILY (LILY)

Smurflily is smart, sassy, and practical. She can be outspoken and at times disagrees with the rest of Smurfy Grove, but she always wants what is best for her sisters.

# BRAINY SMURF'S WALK

When the Smurfs and the girls meet one another for the first time, there's an awkward, distrustful moment...

They observe and criticize one another...

They're weird!

But they look like Smurfette...

But they have funny hairdos. And blue hair!

Those Smurfs look funny!

Yes, they're dressed smurfly, with their white pants and bare chests...

And they don't have hair!

Then curiosity wins out...

Anyhow, we've never seen female smurfs. It gives me a funny feeling!

I think they're kind of pretty!

Oh, yeah?

Someone takes the first step...

The one with the glasses looks funny.

What if we invited him to smurf a walk with us?

Oh, yes, good idea! Heeheehee! I'll see to it!

Hello, you! So, what's your name? I'm Smurfblossom!

Uh...my name's Brainy Smurf!

Well now, I guess that makes you a real smarty-pants! Heeheehee!

Would you like to smurf a walk with my friends and me?

Uh...Yes, I would!

1

What? They're going off with Brainy Smurf?

Very weird!

Uh, yes... They noticed my superiority right away!

A superior smurfache, yes!

They're going to kick themselves for inviting him.

We have tons and tons of activities. We never get bored! And how do you smurf your days in your village?

Well... Often, there's work to be smurfed. We repair the bridge or the dam. Or else, we go smurf fruits and berries in the forest...

And we love to smurf parties. We eat, sing, and dance the whole evening!

Oh, yeah, us, too!

Show us how you all dance!

Certainly!

Here goes. I smurf myself into position.

Tralalaaa smurflala...

Tralalaaa...

Smurf-lalaaaaa!

Ah, okay... Not terrible!

10

Come on, girls! It's our turn to smurf him a demonstration.

Yeaaah! I'll run and get my instrument!

Ready? Here goes!

Okay, come dance with us!

Uh... I don't think I--

Whoa! Ouch!

I don't think he has a knack for our dancing!

Oww! My neck! My back!

Don't you smurf! We'll look after it!

Come in, I'll take care of you.

Smurf onto the table. Come on, don't be afraid!

First, some essential vine oil... It's excellent for your joints!

Oh! That smurfs!... I mean, it has a strong odor!

And now, the most effective thing...

A massage?

No, I'm going to smurf our sucker beetle on your back!

AAAH!

No reason to! I feel much better!

Well, his cure was smurfly fast!

We also smurf a lot of exercise. Do you want to try?

No, thanks! Not at the moment!

Then, could we go smurf a walk in the forest?

Yes, that's a good idea!

To smurf for our outings, we always take our bows and arrows.

They're for defending ourselves. If someone attacks us, we knock out our adversary. Heeheehee!

Like this; look!

ZING

POK

Not bad! I'm a champion, too, at bow and arrows!

Show us!

Wow! What style!

BAP

OWW!

Who smurfed that arrow?

狗!

Smurfstorm's the one who got smurfed!

The way she is, you'd better run fast, champ! Heeheehee!

M-my glasses were fogged up!

Now, let's go smurf on your camouflage!

What?

Yes, you saw: we never go out without camouflage.

Everything you need is here!

Why yes, of course!

I could see him with this one.

It's a little small!

Ah, look...This one will do the job!

Nice!

Is this really necessary?

Absolutely, it's a security measure. Don't move, I'll put your glasses back on.

It's perfect like that!

Wait, wait! Let's smurf an original touch...

5

13

Yes! You made a great smurf with that!

It's awesome!

But I can't go out like this!

And why not? It looks smurf on you!

Just wait long enough for us to camouflage ourselves, too, and we'll go!

Let's go!

Oh! Look at that!

Brainy Smurf! We didn't recognize you...

You're looking smurfly good in that outfit!

Keep moving, keep moving! No dragging around!

?

To smurf in the forest, we'll set out from up there.

From here? But how--?

Easy, you just smurf from vine to vine.

You'll see, it's really smurf!

6

Hup, we're off!

YIPPEE!

Uh, yes... Yippee!

Heeheehee!

And whoahooo!

And whoa--

AAAAHH

Oh, he fell!

Don't you smurf, everything's okay. The plant broke my fall!

Ah, yes... That's good for the fall. But that plant is a smurfulus with stinging hairs.

A WHAT?

Yikes! Oww! It burns! Smurf me out of here!

We're coming!

You're better off on solid ground!

15

Aaaaah, it's awful! It's smurfing me all over!

Come this way. We have a completely natural cure.

You just have to take a nice mud bath in the stinky swamp.

Well? Has the itching stopped?

Yes, but this is gross!

A nice shower under the Crystal Falls will fix that!

AAAAH! It's fre--fre--freezing!

Later, at the village...

So, is it true, you're leaving us already?

Yes, I need to smurf a little rest. Thanks for the lovely walk.

Ahh, our sweetheart is already back. But he looks terrible!

Yes! Hanging out with girls looks smurfly exhausting.

If you only knew!

AAATCHOO!

Hey, your friend's tired already, but not us.

Do you want to go take a walk together?

Uh...it's already late.

Yes, we'd better smurf this off until tomorrow!

♪Pfft!♪ Those Smurfs don't know how to have fun!

END

# CHALLENGES FOR HEFTY SMURF

One morning, at Smurfy Grove, the girls' village...

Gargamel had captured Smurfette and had smurfed her into a cage! Undeterred by the danger, I went, alone, to challenge that infernal sorcerer...

Ooooh!

Oooh!

⸸Pff⸸...What baloney!

Alone against Gargamel, eh? I wish I could've smurfed that with my own eyes!

!

Go ahead and say I'm talking nonsense! Hefty Smurf is no liar!

Your famous sorcerer Gargawhatsit, well, I, Smurfstorm, would've smurfed him a spanking in no time at all!

Gargamel is the Smurfs' greatest enemy! You must be very brave to confront him!

Bah! He's surely not the equal of a Gobble-All!

A Gobble-All? What's that?

It'll guzzle a Smurf like you for breakfast! You're no match for it!

Well, I'd like to see that!

Bah, in any case, I'm sure that we girls are as brave as you Smurfs... if not more!

OH, YEAH!? WANT TO BET?

YEAH! LET'S BET!

2

Did you hear that, girls? He challenged me!

Oh, yesssss! A challenge!

It's gonna be smurftastic!

Yeaaaah!

?

Why do I have the impression that's exactly what she wanted?

Uhhhhh...

Well? What sort of challenge do you want to smurf?

Well... I don't really know! You choose!

Okay, follow me!

She's gonna smurf him down a peg or two!

?

It'll be a laugh!

What's going on?

Hefty Smurf and Stormy have smurfed a challenge! It'll probably be super tough!

A challenge!? What's this all about again?

Soon after, at the edges of the waterfalls bordering the village...

You see that flower over there...? It's a very rare species that grows only on the rocks of the rapids!

The first one to smurf it wins the challenge!...

Of course, whoever falls into the water-- Well, I'll leave that to your imagination...

Courageously braving the waves, Hefty Smurf rushes off without delay...

Hey, Stormy, he's going fast... You're not gonna let him win, are you?

!

!

!

After grabbing a vine, Smurfstorm attaches it to the end of one of the pointed arrows...

4

Then she draws her bow as taut as she can...

...and, with precision, shoots her arrow...

TZING

...into a tree on the other side of the rapids.

TCHAK

Just you wait and smurf!

Look out below!

That goofball doesn't know who he's dealing with!

That's it, I got it!

Come to mama, pretty flower!

!?

N'PLUCK

YAH-HOOOO!
Smurfstorm won!

A few moments later, on the shore...

That's not fair, you cheated!

Me? Come on, nobody ever said how you were supposed to pick this flower!

I'm entitled to a second chance. I want to face a Gobble-All! You'll see who's smurfer!

Okay!

5

Later...

So that's your Gobble-All? Some kind of big onion!?

Just wait!

BOP

FSSSSSSSSSSSSSS...

FSSSSSSSS!

FSSSSSSSSSS!

!?

As its name indicates, a Gobble-All eats everything! Once it catches you, it smurfs you in its belly and you're digested in the blink of an eye...

;Gulp!;

So? Still in a hurry to face it?

Yeah, that's just what I thought...lots of talk...

Hey, what's the deal about a challenge? Papa Smurf certainly won't be happy to--

Don't go there, Brainy Smurf! You're too close to--

FSSSSS

?

6

AAAAH!

FSSSSs.

FSSSSS.....

Brainy Smurf!

He's going to get smurfed alive!

**NO!** There's no way I'm abandoning my friend!

Let him go, you dirty weed!

WAP

!

FSSSSSS

This thing is too strong! I'll never defeat it on my own!

?

WAP

Move out, girls! Let's smurf that Gobble-All!

KAAYAAAAAA!

In no time at all, the carnivorous plant gets a good thrashing...

ZING

And before long, it falls to the blows...

**KAYAAA!**
We smurfed that fat lump!

Thanks for saving us! I have to admit you're really good! You won the two challenges!

Are you kidding? Did you see how you rushed at the monster without hesitating? You have the courage of a warrior, you deserve to be one of us!

SLAP

He can be part of our tribe, can't he, girls?

And how! **KAYAAA!**

Okay, now we're going to smurf a little party... And then, we'll do the initiation rite!

Uhhhhh... What's that? An initiation rite?

?!

END

# CLUMSY SMURF'S DRAGONFLY

One morning, Stormy is training on Spitfire, her dragonfly...

It's smurfly incredible what kind of acrobatics they can smurf!

VOOF

Spitfire! FIRE!

VLOF

WOW! It must be cool having your own dragonfly, Smurfblossom!

Well, you can have one, too, Clumsy Smurf. You just have to earn the trust of one of them!

Oh?

Of course, you'll have to get close to one without being noticed!

Then you'll have to smurf onto its back...

While not getting yourself burned alive!

Afterwards, you grab hold and, if you hold on long enough, maybe you'll become its trusted Smurf!

Say, since you know where their nests can be smurfed, could you take me there?

No way! Willow, our leader, forbids us to go there!

A little later, in the forest...

But you promise it's just to look and that we won't stay long?

Cross my smurf!

Okay! We're here! It's there, just behind this mound!

**WOW!** It's--it's fantasmurf!

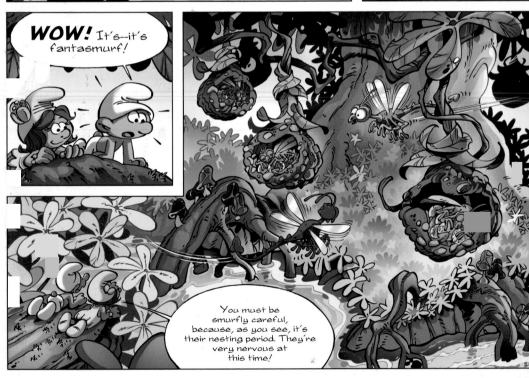

You must be smurfly careful, because, as you see, it's their nesting period. They're very nervous at this time!

You mustn't disturb them when they're roosting.

Oh! Did you see that one? It has only one egg...

That's weird--

--usually, they smurf several of them!

Okay, now let's go back. Willow might realize that we came here!

She'll be very angry and take away our cream smurfs!

You don't want that, do you, Clumsy Smurf?

Not me, anyhow!

Are you listening?

?

I'd just like to be able to smurf an egg to see what it looks like.

Clumsy Smurf! **NO!** Don't do that!

ZBOING WAAAH!

POF

!?

Heh heh heh...

27

Furious at the presence of this intruder, the dragonfly takes off and an aerial rodeo ensues...

**HEY!**

**EEEEEK!**

Clumsy Smurf hangs onto the furious insect's back as best he can...

**WAAH!**

But in its attempts to dislodge her rider, the dragonfly collides with its nest...

**BOK**

...and knocks out its only egg!

**Oops!**

**eeeK?**

The dragonfly dives to try to save its egg...

In vain. The latter disappears into the river waters...

**HEY!**

**PLOOSH**

As does Clumsy Smurf!

**SPLASH**

It's a **CATASMURFRE!** The river will carry him away!

**HELP!** The current's too strong!

**AAAAH--**

Oh, no! The river's carrying him into that cavern!

I must alert Willow! We're sure gonna be in smurf! You can kiss that cream smurf goodbye!

In the meantime, somewhere underground...

Where am I?

?

**BRRR!** It's smurfly cold down here. I don't like it...

Luckily the egg's glowing in the dark and lighting my way.

- CRRIT
- CRRIT
- CRRIT...

?

!?

Any-- anybody there?

**RATS! BIG, STARVING RATS!**

Unless I'm mistaken, rats eat eggs!

AND MAYBE EVEN SMURFS!

OOPS!

WAK

WOOAAHHH...

Phew! What a tumble!... I...

THE EGG?! I hope--

Whew! It's intact! Hello? It fell into some sort of tunnel!

I even smell fresh air smurfing. Maybe it leads to the way out!

Clumsy Smurf bravely heads into the narrow passageway!...

And after several hours of forced spelunking...

It's good to see daylight again...

Now I have to resmurf this egg to its mother!

PAT. PAT...

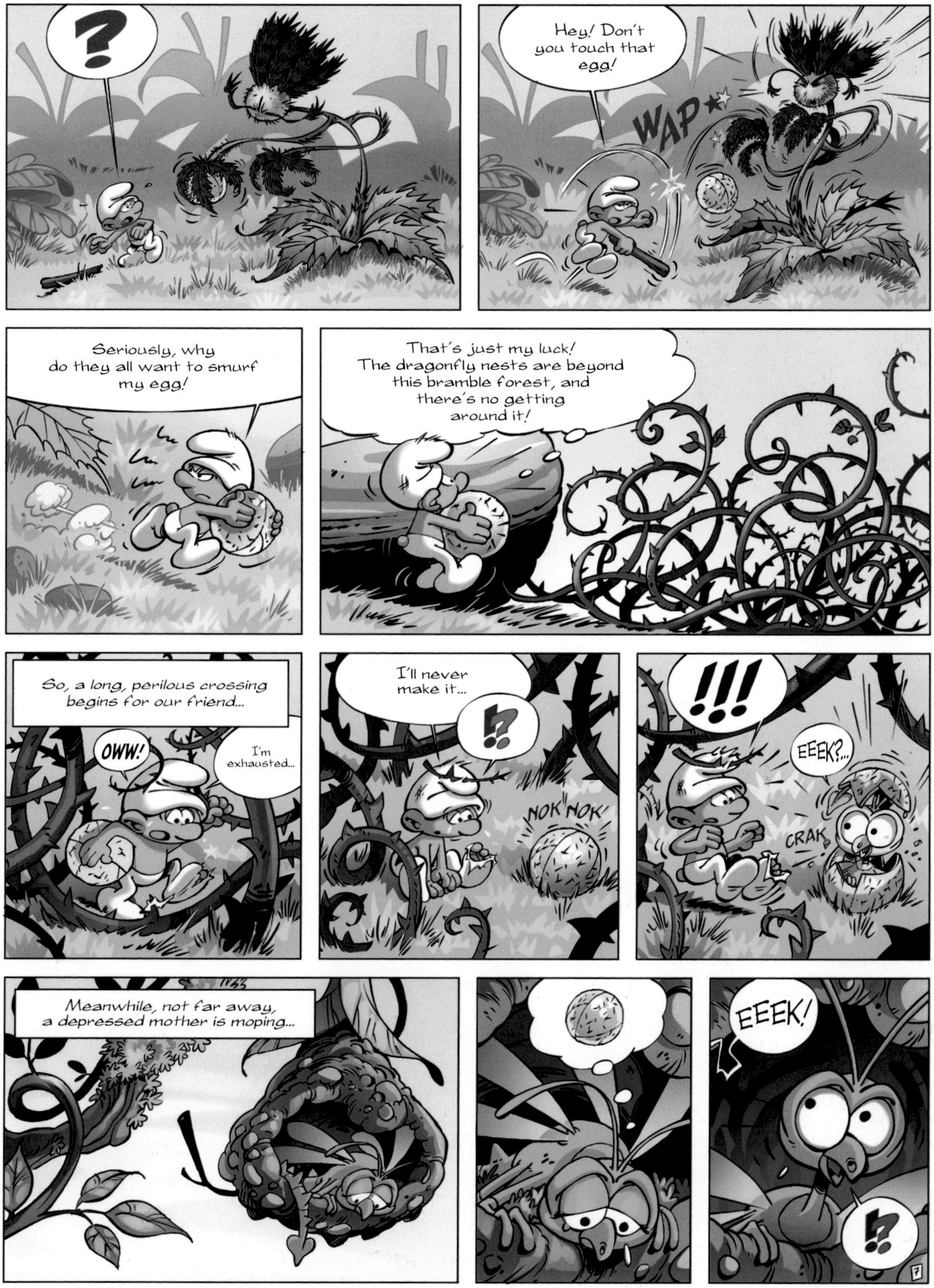
?
Hey! Don't you touch that egg!
WAP
Seriously, why do they all want to smurf my egg!
That's just my luck! The dragonfly nests are beyond this bramble forest, and there's no getting around it!
So, a long, perilous crossing begins for our friend...
OWW!
I'm exhausted...
I'll never make it...
!?
NOK NOK
!!!
EEEK?...
CRAK
Meanwhile, not far away, a depressed mother is moping...
!
EEEK!
!?

EEEEK!...

Uh... How can I be sure she's not still mad at me?

GULP

I can't look!

She's going to smurf me like a marshmallow over a fire...

HEY!

VOOF

Heh heh... You're happy I brought your baby home, is that it? Yes, yes, I love both of you, too!

Clumsy Smurf, is everything okay?

We came to rescue you!

Rescue me? There's no need! Let me smurf my new friends to you instead!

!!!

And since that day, Clumsy Smurf can be seen riding his own dragonfly...

You go! You're the best, Looping!

END

# THE SQUASH SMURFS

Today, Smurfwillow has brought the Smurf's to the harvest...

Here's our field of squash!

They're the base of our entire dietary smurf!

You can smurf them in soups, in pies, in cakes...

We do the same thing with sarsaparilla!

Here! Have a taste! I bet you'll like it!

Yum!... ♪hmmm♪...It's-- Yum!... Smurfly good!

**WILLOW! WILLOW!**
The squash smurfer has busted everything again like the last time!

1

OH!

Look! All our work is smurfed!

It's him again, I recognize his footprints!

And these are the same blue hairs. We found them stuck to thorns!

This can't go on, Willow! We must smurf a solution!

You're right, Stormy!

Who smurfed your squash?

We don't know! For some time now, an animal's been coming to steal from us and smash everything. But the blue hairs and those prints don't belong to any animal of the enchanted forest!

Why don't you lay a trap for him?

You're right, Smurfette! Smurfstorm, assemble everyone and smurf what's necessary!

We're gonna kick his butt!

We'll smurf you a hand!

Soon after...

There, Willow. We've smurfed some squash as a lure!

Once it grabs one, this rope will release...

And this cage will drop on the dirty, thieving smurf!

Perfect, Stormy! Tonight, we'll finally know who our squash smurfer is!

That night, threatening silhouettes keep watch, hidden in the underbrush...

Do you really think it'll come, Stormy?

It always comes back to the scene of its crime!

!

KRAK

Shhhhh!... I thought I heard something...

BLANG
CRAC

!

Attack! Smurf it!

KAYAAA!

Move out, Smurfs! Let's go see that thief's mug!

**WHAT?!** What is that smurf?

3

Have you ever seen anything like that, Willow?

GROOO!

Never! Even in the book of the Elders, I don't think I've ever seen any animal of the kind!

HEY! LOOK OUT! Th-that thing's going to get out!

GROOOAAAAAA

CRAC

You big oaf, I'll calm you down!

BOP

GROAAAR!

One day we'll have to talk about your way of calming things down, Blossom!

4

Let me put this on one of your arrows, Stormy! This powder I made is a very powerful sleeping agent!

Now, go ahead, aim for its snout!

?!

POOF

KOFF
KOFF

Under the effect of the powder, the animal soon begins to stagger...

And ends up falling down fast asleep...

ZZZ

PLOPP

Go find some bamboo stems. We'll make a stretcher and carry it to the village!

ZZZ

A short time afterward, a strange procession sets out...

ZZZ

Later, at the village...

What will we do with it?

We'll assemble the council to decide its fate!

The council?

ZZZ

Important decisions concerning the village are always quickly decided collectively in a council!

37

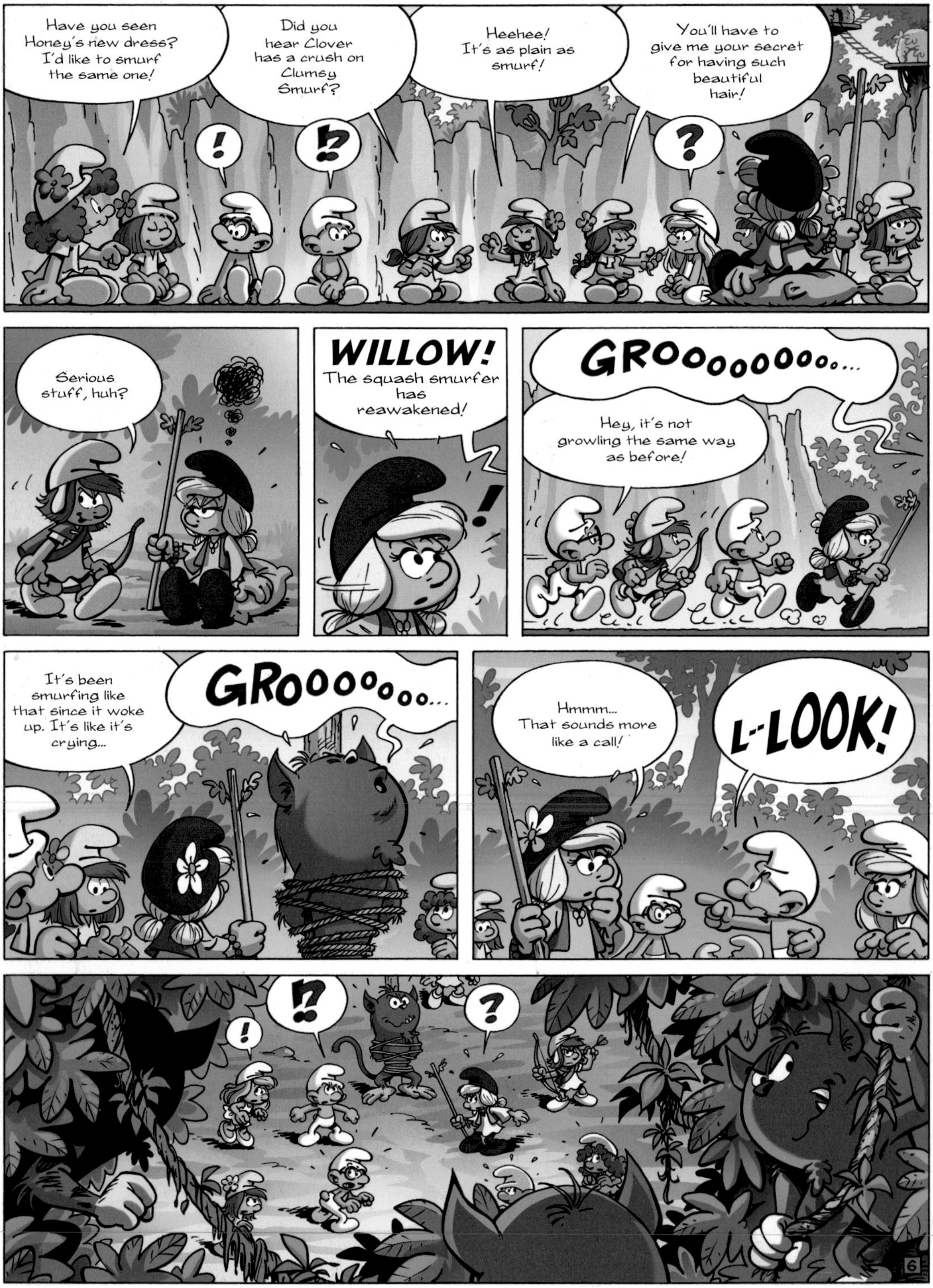
Have you seen Honey's new dress? I'd like to smurf the same one!
!
Did you hear Clover has a crush on Clumsy Smurf?
!?
Heehee! It's as plain as smurf!
You'll have to give me your secret for having such beautiful hair!
?
Serious stuff, huh?
WILLOW! The squash smurfer has reawakened!
!
GROOOOOOOOOO...
Hey, it's not growling the same way as before!
It's been smurfing like that since it woke up. It's like it's crying...
GROOOOOOOO...
Hmmm... That sounds more like a call!
L-LOOK!
!
!?
?
6

There's an immediate panic!

The Growler's friends are attacking us! Run for your smurfs!

All throughout the village, the creatures create chaos...

GROOAAA!

Destroying everything in their path...

BASH

Hey, there! You peeping smurf!

There's no way they're destroying my hives! Please, someone help me!

Stormy! Come with me! I have an idea!

!

GACK!

Hey! Careful! You'll get the bees mad!

That's the goal!

BZzzz...

BZzz

Hey! You Growlers there! This way!

?!

?

BZzzz

Upsy-daisy!

GROOO?!

The Growlers are soon routed...

Ha! Ha! One little sting and they hightail it like rabbits!

Well done, Hefty Smurf!

KAYAAA!

We chased them away, but we'll have to be wary of these newcomers to our forest!

I think you're right, Stormy! We haven't heard the last of those Growlers!

They did nonetheless manage to free their friend!

Good riddance!

END

8

# A SMURFLILY STRANGE WORLD

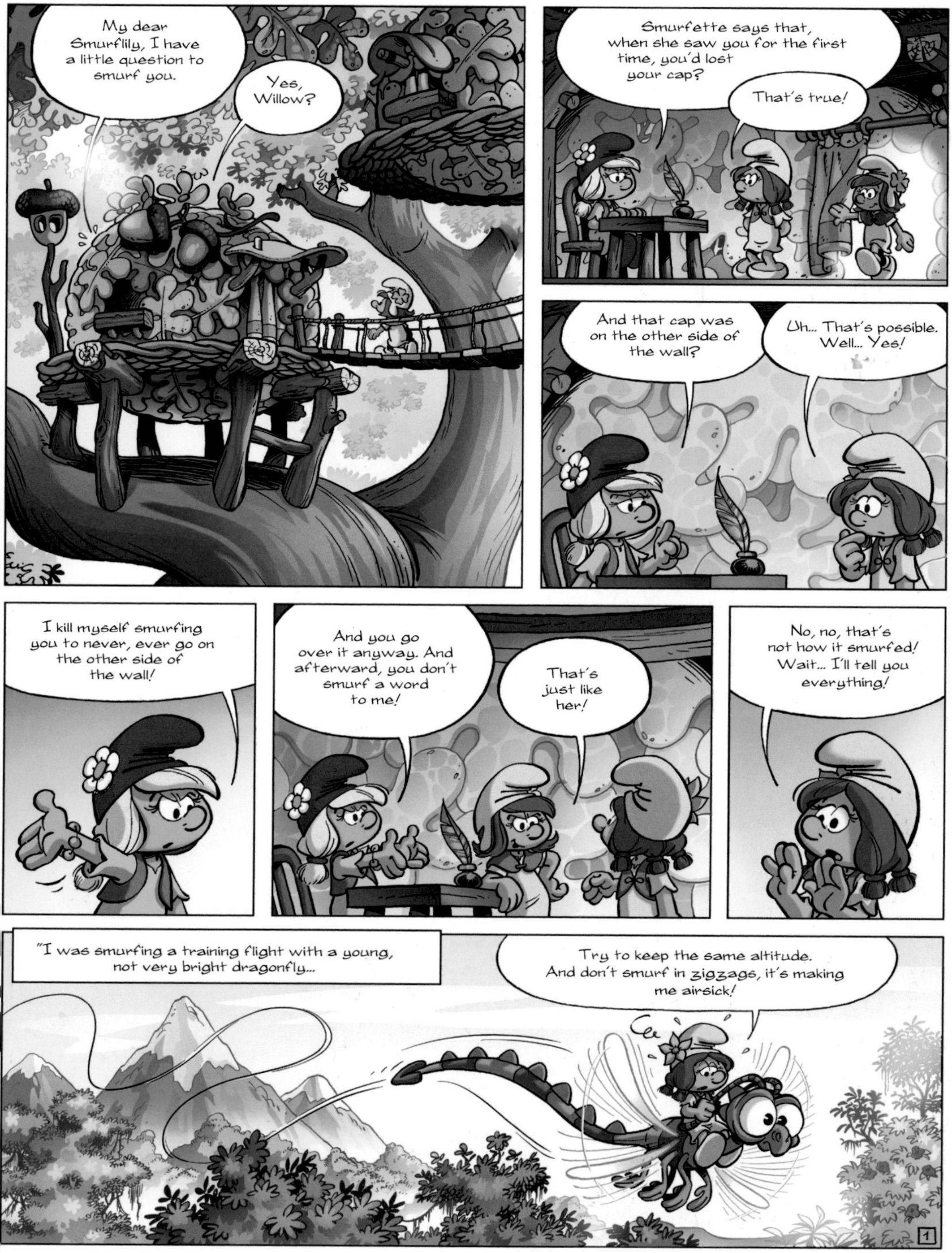

My dear Smurflily, I have a little question to smurf you.
Yes, Willow?
Smurfette says that, when she saw you for the first time, you'd lost your cap?
That's true!
And that cap was on the other side of the wall?
Uh... That's possible. Well... Yes!
I kill myself smurfing you to never, ever go on the other side of the wall!
And you go over it anyway. And afterward, you don't smurf a word to me!
That's just like her!
No, no, that's not how it smurfed! Wait... I'll tell you everything!
"I was smurfing a training flight with a young, not very bright dragonfly...
Try to keep the same altitude. And don't smurf in zigzags, it's making me airsick!
1

Okay, I think that's enough for today. Let's smurf back to the village!

Huh?

Where are you smurfing? The village isn't that way! Hey, do you hear me?

The wall! We're coming to the wall!

You must never smurf beyond the wall! Turn around, right now!

Whoa!

NO! Not through the--

--plants!

COME BACK! COME BACK RIGHT NOW!

AND STOP SMURFING AT ME LIKE THAT, YOU CREEPS!

I can't believe it! That nitwit doesn't even realize he's smurfed me going through?

GLOB

*EEEEEE!* Let go! Let go! Let go!

WAP WAP WAP

PTOOEY

?

BOING

PLOP

Oh! There he is! *HELP! I'M HERE!*

Yoohoo! Come back! Smurf me out of here!

It's no smurf, he didn't hear me!

I'll have to smurf out of here on my own.

3

I don't even know anymore which direction I must smurf!

SMOOCH

Smurf me in peace, you! Now's not the time!

Mind your manners!

I think it's this way!

We girls have an innate sense of direction!

Finally, some light! I think I'll smurf out of this jungle!

Oh, no!

I'm at the foot of the wall!

I must have smurfed in a circle! And now I'm exhausted...

What's more, the scent of all these flowers is smurfing to my head... I have to... rest a little...

4

44

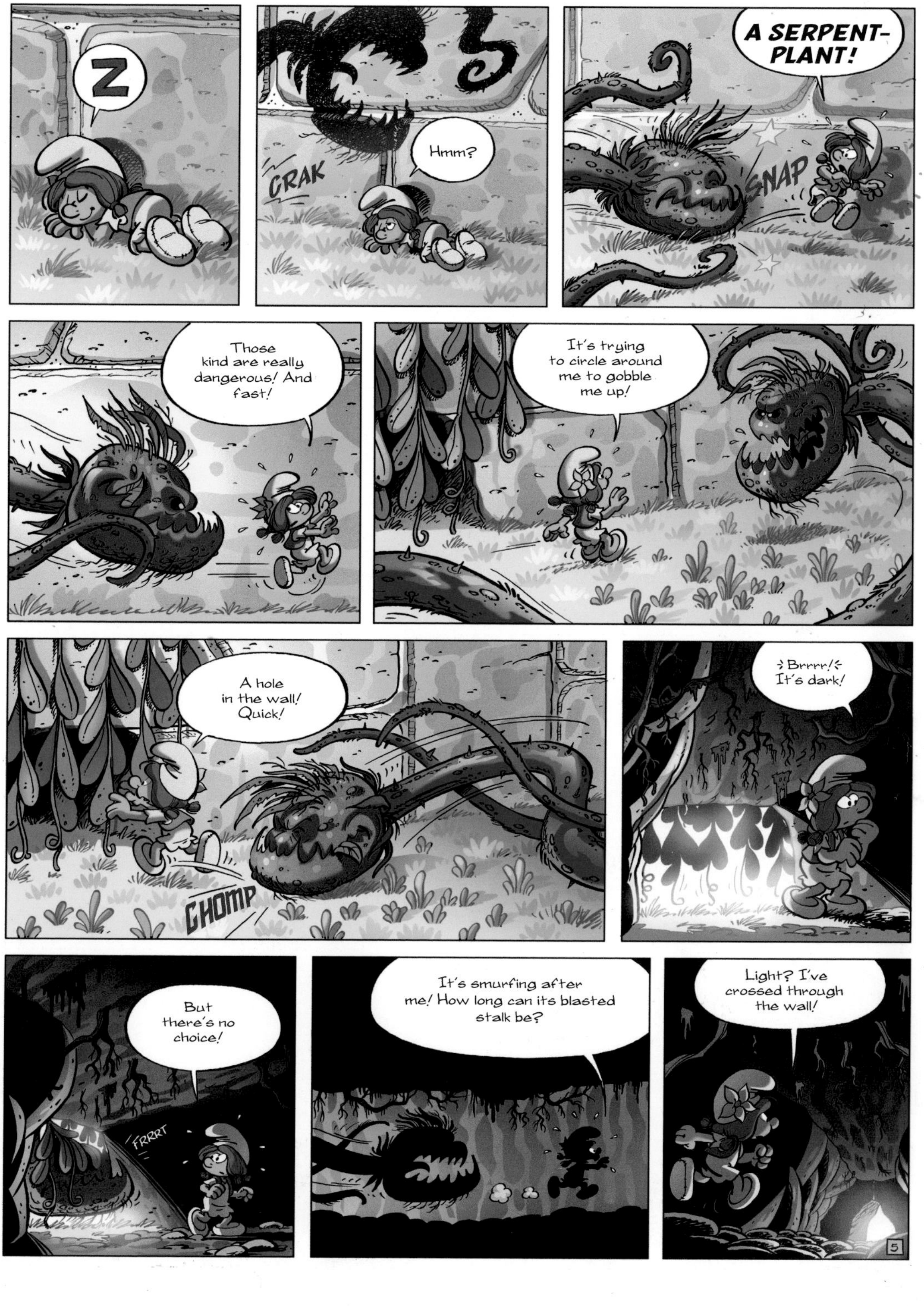
Z
CRAK
Hmm?
A SERPENT-PLANT!
SNAP
Those kind are really dangerous! And fast!
It's trying to circle around me to gobble me up!
A hole in the wall! Quick!
CHOMP
Brrrr! It's dark!
But there's no choice!
FRRRT
It's smurfing after me! How long can its blasted stalk be?
Light? I've crossed through the wall!
5

OOOH!

I-It's not at all like our home here!

SNAP

Yikes, I forgot about the serpent-plant!

Not coming any farther, eh? Are you afraid of smurfing yourself, you big scaredy-cat?

No, it's because its stalk is too short.

Serves you right! SPRTZ

SNAP

What a strange world! It smurfs shivers down my spine.

EEEE!

?

BROOSH

46

That sounded like... a Smurf kind of voice! Here? That's impossible.

The noise was smurfing from there...

Oh!

Yikes! Smurf-kiting in the branches of a tree is a dangerous sport!

What--?! Someone's there!

Hey, who are you? Show yourself!

I'm dreaming! No, I'm hallucinating! I got to smurf back home!

Well, smurf it all! You're still here?

SNAP!

Are you finally going to smurf me in peace?

You're hungry, is that it?

Eat up then!

7

You'd better spit it out. That's hard to digest!

‡ Whew! ‡ I'm back in the normal world now. I'm safe!

"So, I smurfed along the wall to a path I know well and I came home."

Afterwards, I thought I'd dreamt it all! Do you realize, I'd seen a Smurf like us, but with long **BLOND** hair!

Yes, in fact, that does seem like a hallucination!

Well, you're excused for smurfing past the wall. Those were extenuating circumstances.

I say we block up that hole in the wall. It's a danger for us!

You're right, no doubt.

But... without the passage, we'd have never met the Smurfs from beyond! And, if we block it up, they won't be able to come visit us!

It's true, that would be sad! We'll leave the passage open, then.

But you're not allowed to go near it! Or to smurf on the other side of the wall! Understood?

Yes, Willow!

We promise, Willow!

END

8

48

# WATCH OUT FOR PAPERCUTZ™

Welcome to THE SMURFS "The Village Behind the Wall," the graphic novel with five all-new stories featuring the new Smurfs introduced in the *Smurfs: The Lost Village*, the hit movie from Sony Animation. I'm Jim Salicrup, the Editor-in-Chief of Papercutz, the official North American publisher of THE SMURFS comics. Papercutz is dedicated to publishing great graphic novels for all ages, and that obviously includes THE SMURFS!

While this particular graphic novel may include characters, such as Smurfwillow and Smurfstorm, who first appeared in the movie, did you know that THE SMURFS, like Batman, Teenage Mutant Ninja Turtles, Doctor Strange, and countless other movie franchises, first appeared in comics? In other words, this isn't really a comicbook tie-in to a movie or TV property, this is a comics property that has been successfully adapted in many forms of media—film, animation, video games, live shows, and more.

Sometimes comics characters change in such media adaptations, and many new characters suddenly appear as well. For example, Superman didn't really fly until he was animated in a series of cartoons produced by the Fleischer Studios, Batgirl didn't exist until she was created for the live-action Batman TV series in the late 60s, and several popular Smurfs characters, such as Puppy and Grandma Smurf, were invented for the 80s animated TV series. Likewise, the new female Smurfs made their debut in *Smurfs: The Lost Village*. But contrary to popular belief, Smurfette wasn't the only female Smurf prior to the latest *Smurfs* movie — there was the aforementioned Grandma Smurf, as well as Sassette of the Smurflings! But we're getting ahead of ourselves. While this book features the newest SMURFS comics ever published in North America, let's go back to where it all started…

In 1958, a young cartoonist, Pierre Culliford, working under the pen name Peyo (a nickname given to him by a cousin of his), was writing and drawing a light-hearted medieval adventure comic strip called *Johan et Pirlouit* (Johan and Peewit, in our English version) for the legendary Belgian comics magazine, *Spirou*. Johan was a royal page, and sort of a knight-in-training, and Peewit was the court jester. In a story entitled, *La flute à six trous*, ("The Flute with Six Holes"), our heroes, on a mission to find a magical flute, find a village of blue elves known as *les Schtroumpfs*, or, as they've become to be known in English, The Smurfs. Those minor characters, appearing on just 21 pages of a 60-page story, wound up stealing the show from Johan and Peewit, and went on to appear in a graphic novel series of their own, which continues to this day.

Interestingly, the very first time a Smurf appears in the Johan and Peewit story, it's not unlike how we were first introduced to the latest batch of Smurfs in "The Lost Village." All we see are a couple of eyes, hidden behind a few leaves. Funny how one way or another we keep going from the present to the past of THE SMURFS.

But Johan isn't mistaken. Through the foliage, two tiny eyes are watching them ride away.

A Smurf from the Village in Front of the Wall!

Cover from the French edition of this graphic novel.

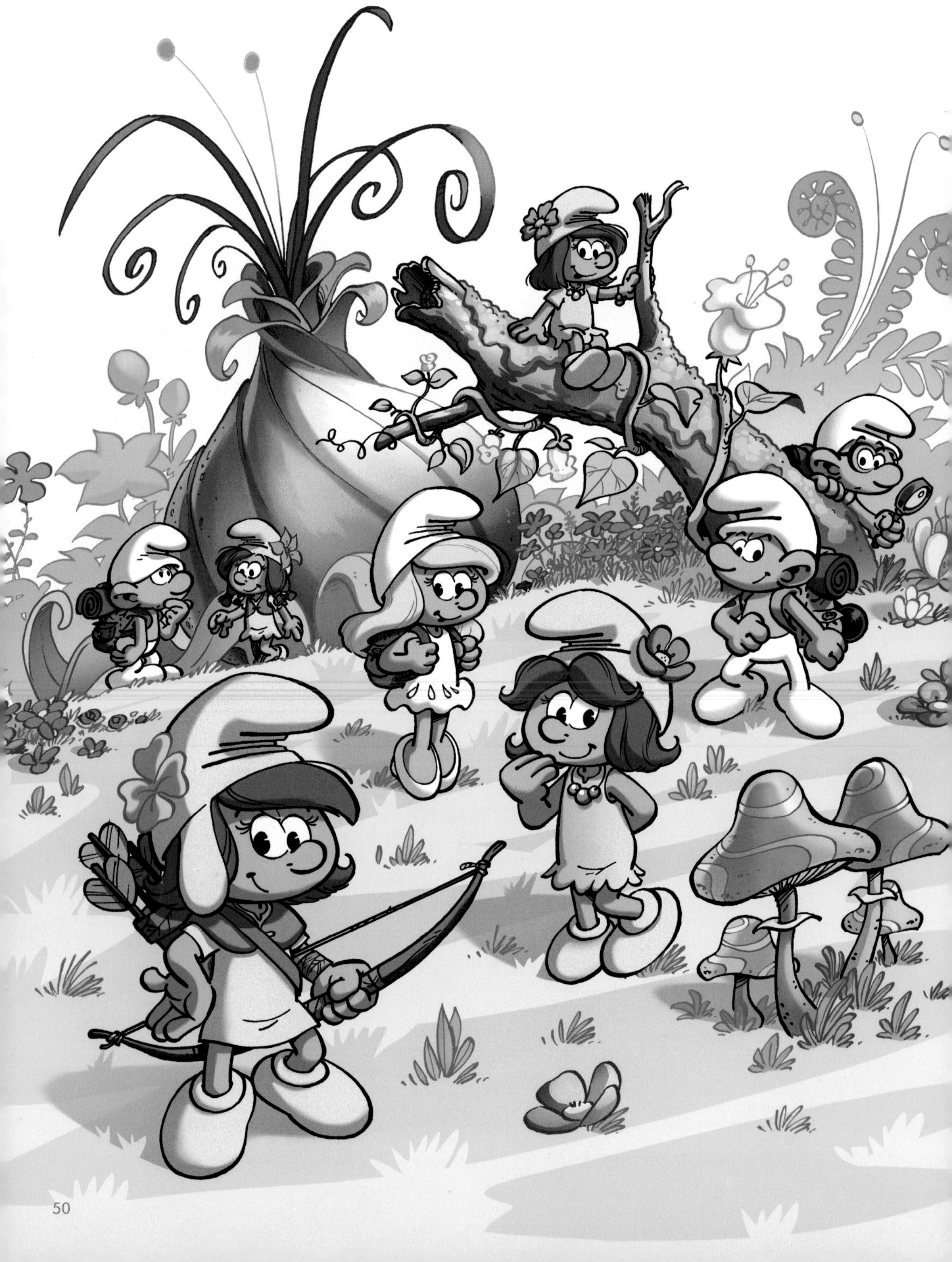

Left: One of Peyo's first drawings of a Smurf. Right: Benny Breakiron, recently the star of his own movie adapting "The Red Taxis."

On the following pages we offer an excerpt from that classic tale, as we see our daring duo sent to the "Cursed Land," where they encounter the Smurfs for the first time. You can get the full story either in THE SMURFS #2 "The Smurfs and the Magic Flute" or THE SMURFS ANTHOLOGY Volume One, both from Papercutz. In 2008, a prequel to that classic tale was created to celebrate the 50th anniversary of THE SMURFS, and it was published by Papercutz in THE SMURFS & FRIENDS Volume One.

Peyo, was nothing if not productive. Before he created THE SMURFS and even Johan and Peewit, he did a comic strip about a cat—a sort of precursor of Gargamel's pet Azrael—called Poussy, or as we dubbed it in English, PUSSYCAT. Much closer in style to conventional newspaper comic strips, most PUSSYCAT strips are a few panels devoted to the telling of a single gag. Yet Peyo's clear story-telling style and gentle humor is evident in every strip – from the earliest crudely drawn strips to the polished later strips drawn by the Peyo studio artists. Papercutz is devoted to publishing as much of Peyo's work as possible, in beautiful editions, and all the PUSSYCAT strips have finally been collected in one volume in English.

Inspired by the success of Superman decades earlier, Peyo put his spin on super heroes with the creation of *Benoit Brisefer*, or as we call him, Benny Breakiron. The story of a small, polite French boy with super-strength, except if he catches a cold, was set in the time period of the '60s, the first story appearing in 1960. There's a strong 60s sensibility pervading the BENNY BREAKIRON strips, with stories spoofing everything from James Bond to evil robots. Papercutz has published four volumes of BENNY BREAKIRON, and BENNY is also featured in THE SMURFS & FRIENDS.

And of course, Papercutz has been publishing THE SMURFS, both in an ongoing series of graphic novels, in large collections such as THE SMURFS ANTHOLOGY and THE SMURFS & FRIENDS, and in special editions such as this one. We're at a special time in this country, where finally great comic art is getting the respect it deserves. Bookstores and comic shop shelves are virtually overflowing with comics treasuries and omnibuses filled with great classic comics, and we're thrilled that the work of Peyo is also included on those shelves.

Unfortunately, on Christmas Eve 1992, Pierre "Peyo" Culliford passed away due to a heart attack. While Peyo may no longer be with us, his joyous spirit lives on, both in SMURFS: The Lost Village and in all THE SMURFS graphic novels.

**STAY IN TOUCH!**
EMAIL: Salicrup@papercutz.com
WEB: www.papercutz.com
TWITTER: @papercutzgn
FACEBOOK: PAPERCUTZGRAPHICNOVELS
SNAIL MAIL: Papercutz, 160 Broadway,
  Suite 700, East Wing, New York, NY 10038

The... the what?

The Smurfs! They're the ones who make the magic flutes!

Oh? Then these... er... Smurfs... could help us!

Yes! It's only, well!...They live in the "Cursed Land!" No road leads there! You have to cross raging torrents flowing through deep gorges with steep embankments! To cross the swamps oozing deadly vapors! There are forests infested with serpents! Quicksand! No, believe me! Nobody ever makes it to the Cursed Land!

Nevertheless, there's one thing I could try for you! Send you there by hypno-kinesis! What do you think of that?

Well...

Er...

Very well! Come! We'll attempt the experiment right away!

Sit there!

Wh-what are you going to do to us? No jokes, okay?

Of course not! I'm simply going to put you to sleep and...

AGAIN?! It's becoming a habit! Falling asleep is all that we ever do anymore!

Shhh! Hush now!

You'll be plunged into a lethargic sleep! Then, thanks to certain magical formulas, I'll split your personality and I'll make it rematerialize in the Cursed Land! You'll be here, but in fact, you'll be there! Do you understand?

Absolutely nothing!

It doesn't matter! Look deep into my eyes! Relax! Don't think of anything!

Let yourself go! You must sleep! Sleep! Sleep! Sleep! Sleep!

Wh-where's Homnibus? Where are we?

In the Cursed Land!

You think? It's not very nice here!

And where are those legendary Smurfs?

It's strange! There is no dwelling of any kind to be seen!

It's sinister here!

What a strange country!

For smurf's sake! Can't you watch where you put your smurfs? You nearly smurfed me!

Why it's Johan and Peewit! That's quite a smurf! What are you two smurfing here?

What? You know us?

Of course! When you still had the smurf with six smurfs, we tried to smurf it back from you, but...

What? Excuse us, but we don't understand anything that you're saying!

Oh! That's right! You don't smurf smurf!

Smurf after me! I'm going to smurf you to Papa Smurf's!

Do you understand any of that gibberish?

No! But I think he's signaling for us to follow him!

Where's he taking us?

I don't know! To his friends, no doubt!

I hope they don't keep saying "smurfs" and "smurfing," otherwise it won't be easy making them understand what we want!

We're here!

Look! Two smurfs!

What are they smurfing here?

They sure look smurfy!

Ah! There's Papa Smurf... the big smurf!

If he's "the big" Smurf, then I'm the Immense Peewit!

Papa Smurf, here are Johan and Peewit!

Aha!

Welcome! But how did you get here? I thought it was impossible!

We can understand you, at least!

It was the Magician Homnibus who put us to sleep, and we awoke here!

Oh! I see! Er, could you bend down a little? I'm going to get a stiff neck! Actually— hold on!

Smurf over here!

So smurf elsewhere, you smurfs!

But... Papa Smurf, we don't...

What's that I have to smurf seriously with two smurfs! Get going! Scram!

Oh, those kids! Just because they're a hundred years old, they think they can do anything!

?

What? They're a hundred?

And you say that they're children?! But how old are you, then?

I was 542 years old at the mushroom harvest!

**542 YEARS!!?**
Uh... you don't look it!

Let's cut to the chase! You didn't succeed in getting the flute with six holes back from that crooked Oilycreep and you've come to ask us for our help! Right?

38

Uh... yes! But how do you know all that?

Simple! We heard that a merchant had found one of our flutes in the ashes of the cottage of the sorcerer to whom we'd given it!

As it couldn't remain in the wrong hands, my smurfs set out on a hunt to recover it!

Thus it was that, the day when the merchant lost it, you're the ones whom they secretly followed, until Oilycreep stole it from you! You never guessed, eh?

So now they're tracking Oilycreep, waiting for an inattentive moment, which will let them snatch the flute back! But I'm not very hopeful, for the fellow is both mistrustful and crafty!

But isn't there any way to break the flute's enchantment? That would fix everything!

No! It's impossible!

Too bad! Come on, all we can do is to resume our pursuit of that brigand!

What's the idea of making such flutes? You see all the problems we have now because of you?

What if we gave you the means to fight with equal armaments?

What do you mean?

We could make you ANOTHER flute with six holes!

That's a brilliant idea!

Great Googa Mooga! That's the solution! How long before we could have it?

Wait! Hey! Smurf!

How much smurf do you need to smurf a new smurf with six smurfs?

Oh! By smurfing hard, you'd have to smurf on three smurfs!

He says we must figure on three days! Come! There's not a moment to lose! To work!

33

For the whole story see THE SMURFS #2 "The Smurfs and the Magic Flute" or THE SMURFS ANTHOLOGY VOL. 1

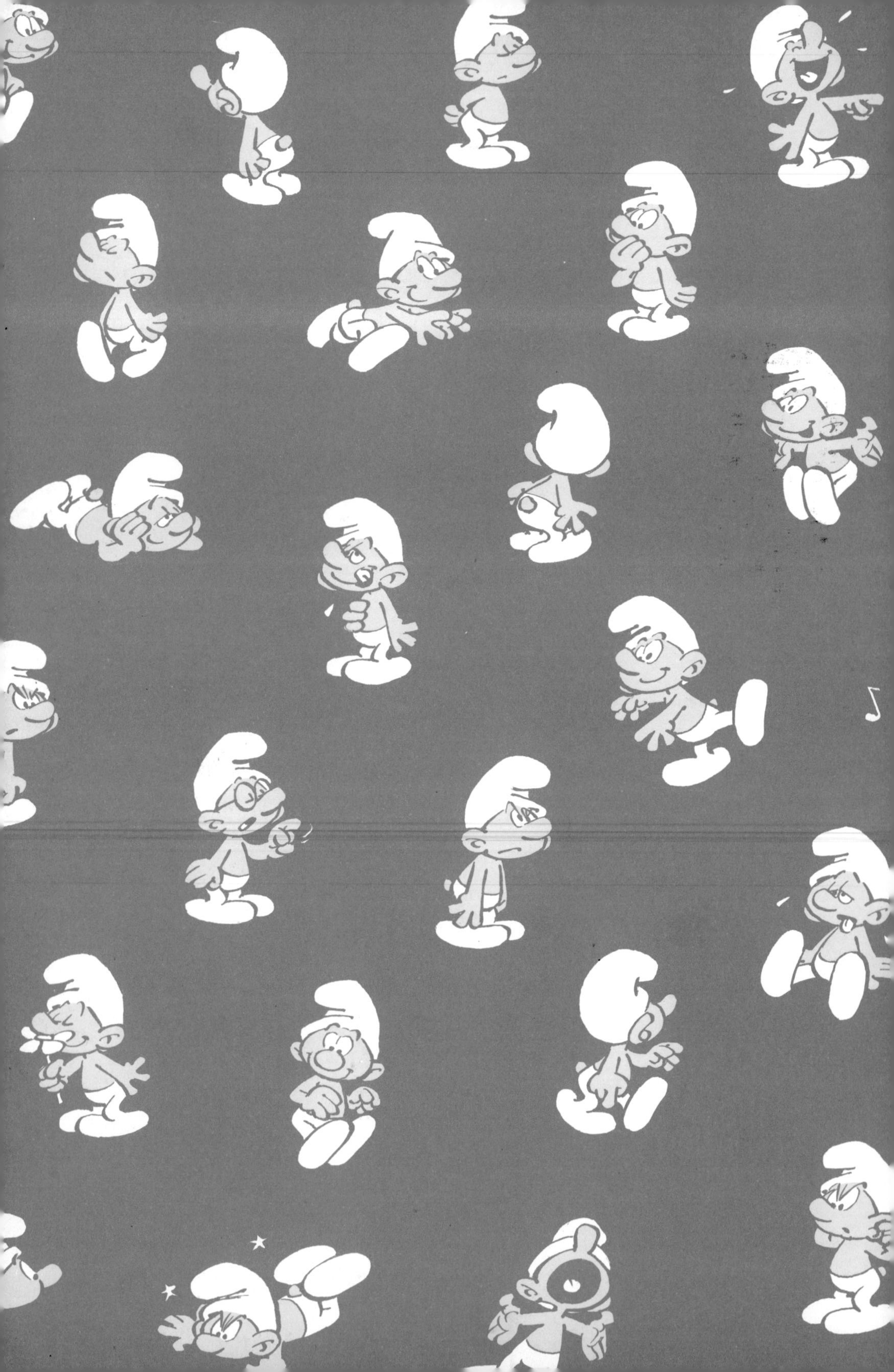